£4.45

Printed and Published by D. C. Thomson & Co., Ltd.,
Dundee and London

Hello, girls!

Here's another super, fun-packed Twinkle Book specially for *YOU!*

Inside, you'll meet all your favourite Twinkle chums - Nurse Nancy, *Patch,* Silly Milly, Honey and *Sally and Scamp* - AND find plenty of great new stories, too.

You'll love reading *Splish! Splash!* and Wonderful Wonderland, as well as having a terrific time with lots of games and puzzles.

There are 64 full colour pages for you to enjoy.

Have fun!

Love,

Twinkle.

Nurse Nancy

1 — Nancy is the nurse at the Dollies Hospital. It was nearly Christmas time, so Nancy and Colin, the ambulance boy, decided to put up the hospital decorations.

2 — The patients in the ward were excited and joined in the fun. Toby the teddy helped by holding a string of baubles ready for Nancy to add to the tree.

3 — Most of the patients were going home for Christmas and, as Nancy wheeled two through, she heard Grandad on the phone. "Yes. We can help you, Mr Jones," he said.

4 — After Nancy waved goodbye, Grandad told her that the toy factory manager had called for help. "Their specialist dolls' machinery has broken down," he said.

5 — Grandad took Nancy and Colin along to the toy factory. "I may be a while," he said. "Wow!" gasped Colin. "I've *always* wanted to visit a toy factory!"

6 — "It's *brilliant*!" agreed Nancy. "I hope Grandad talks to the manager for *ages*!" she chuckled. "I could look round here for ever. There are so many toys!"

7 — Soon Grandad returned, though, and he told Nancy that they had one *hundred* special dolls to put together. Nancy and Colin helped load the car.

8 — "These are the kind of dolls they made when I was a boy," Grandad told Nancy and Colin later. "Mr Jones knew that I would be able to fasten on the parts."

9 — "The dolls will need clothes when Grandad has put them together," thought Nancy. And she set to work sewing.

10 — Colin set up a conveyer belt — just like in the toy factory — and the Dollies Hospital team worked together to dress and pack the dolls. "They'll be ready for Christmas," said Nancy.

11 — As a reward, Nancy and Colin were invited to the toy factory's Christmas party and given super gifts. Nancy's was a walking, talking nurse doll — just like herself!

Silly Milly

She's always in a muddle

1 — Milly was excited — she was going to a Christmas party. "I'm really looking forward to this," she thought. "Colin usually has something *special* at his parties."

2 — Inside, however, everyone looked glum. "I booked an entertainer, but he has had to cancel," explained Colin's mum. "Oh, dear," said Milly. "We can't have sad faces."

3 — "*I'll* sort things," Milly offered. "We'll start off with a game of blind man's buff. You put on the blindfold, Sophie." But Sophie didn't want to. "It's *boring*," she scowled.

4 — Everyone agreed, so Milly decided to take first turn. Of course, the silly miss couldn't see where she was going. She tripped over the cat and burst the balloons. *That* raised a smile.

5 — "I'll help set up food," thought Milly. But she stepped on a toy car and sent her drinks tray flying — all over Colin's mum. *That* produced another chuckle.

6 — The cake landed on Milly's head and fell into her eyes. "Who put out the lights?" wailed Milly as she staggered into the Christmas tree. By then *everyone* was laughing.

7 — The Christmas tree toppled over, bringing the decorations down with it. "Gosh!" gasped Milly as she wiped cake from her eyes. "What's happened? An earthquake?"

8 — Colin and his friends could hardly speak for laughing. "It was no earthquake, Milly, it was *you*," Colin roared. "Who needs to have an entertainer at a party when *you're* a guest?"

Puzzle time

Abigail is wearing Victorian clothes. Lead her through the maze to where she's going.

Which silhouette of Abigail exactly matches her figure?

LOD TEMI
Micsu Hlal

Rearrange the letters to discover Abigail's destination.

Answer —
Old Time Music Hall

Can you find six differences between these performers?

Join the dots and Abigail's transport will be revealed!

Abigail has a *super* time at the show. *You* can join in the fun by colouring in the picture. First, find where the small coloured pictures fit and then look for the six hidden ice cream cones.

Wonderful Wonderland

WONDERFUL WONDERLAND was an extra special place to live. Every day, there were fairs, parades, parties and fun and everyone laughed and sang all the time. Everything was *perfect* !

2 — Even the food in Wonderland was wonderful! The pizzas were *enormous* and the hamburgers were the most mouthwatering hamburgers in the world!

One evening, however, the king was not smiling. He had finished his excellent dinner, the jesters had amused everyone and the musician had played beautiful tunes. But the king was *frowning* !

"Is that a frown on your face?" the queen asked, amazed.

"I don't know," answered the king, grumpily, "but something is very wrong! Bring me my trusted advisers!"

"What is wrong, Your Majesty?" they asked, rushing in. "Isn't Wonderland the most perfect place in the world?"

"Yes!" shouted the king, banging his fist on the table. "Yes! It's perfect! *That's* what's wrong! It's too perfect! I'm fed up with everything being wonderful! I'm *bored* ! I want a *surprise* !"

3 — The advisers set to work and, soon, a crowd of people waited to surprise the king.

Even a goose that laid golden eggs and a rainbow-coloured cake didn't surprise him, however.

"Take them away," he ordered. "They're *perfect* ! That's hardly a surprise!"

Then a young girl appeared at the palace gates.

"Let me try to entertain the king," she said.

"Who are you?" the king's advisers asked.

"I'm Mandy — an apprentice magician," said the little girl. "Let me show you . . ."

4 — Waving her magic wand, she said,
  "Watch me very closely here
  And I will make three doves appear."

But, instead of three doves, an *enormous* fat pink pig appeared.

"A pink dove!" laughed one adviser.

"That can't fly," chuckled the other.

5 — "I'll try again," sighed Mandy, and she chanted,
*"Clouds and sun and stars on high,
Give me something that can fly!"*
The pig suddenly shot off with a surprised look and a squeal and a grunt, up into the air and away amongst the clouds.

Everyone shrieked with laughter.

"Pigs *can* fly!" shouted someone and everyone laughed so much tears ran down their faces.

Again the stern trusted advisers roared at Mandy's mistake.

"Ho, ho, ho!" they chuckled.

"Oh, dear!" sighed Mandy. "That pig was supposed to save my bacon. I'd better try something else."

6 — Mandy turned to the crowd of people who were still laughing.

"Sorry about that," she said. "Sometimes my spells go wrong. Just watch this next one."

She tossed some magic dust into the air and cried,
*"Abracadabra! Now you'll see
A spell that turns out right for me!"*
Everyone gasped when a burst of stars tumbled down over her head.

"There!" Mandy said proudly. "It worked *that* time!"

Everyone cheered and clapped.

7 — Meanwhile, the sad king heard the laughter and excitement in the courtyard.

"What is going on?" he called.

"It is just a young girl, Your Majesty," answered an adviser. "She wants to be a magician — but she is not suitable to be brought before Your Majesty."

"There is laughter and fun outside," the king roared crossly, "so I *demand* to see what is happening!"

8 — In a flurry of excitement, Mandy was taken to the king.

"Please show me what you can do, little girl," he said.

Mandy thought for a moment, then whispered,

"Wizards above, I wish and dream
To see before me a pitcher of cream!"

9 — Suddenly, a black and white cow landed before the king and mooed loudly.

The astonished king stared at it for a moment, then he began to laugh.

"That *was* a surprise!" he chuckled. "Please do more."

Mandy's mistakes made the king laugh so much, he asked her to stay at the palace.

After that, a frown was never seen again in Wonderful Wonderland.

Merry-go-round

1 — Merry Carter's family own a travelling Victorian merry-go-round. It was the last day of the season.

2 — Merry wasn't too sad the season was at an end, however. While the adults packed away all the stalls, she had great fun playing in the snow and ice with her fairground friends.

3 — But Merry noticed some of the younger children weren't joining in and asked why. "It's too dangerous," replied one.

4 — Merry thought it was sad the small children were missing out. She went to her daddy and told him she had an idea. "Will you help?" she asked.

5 — Mr Carter said he would be happy to help and went to his store. "I haven't used this old coach in years," said Merry's daddy, "I'm pleased now I kept it!"

6 — Daddy fixed runners on the old coach, turning it into a sledge. The little ones were able to have great fun — in safety!

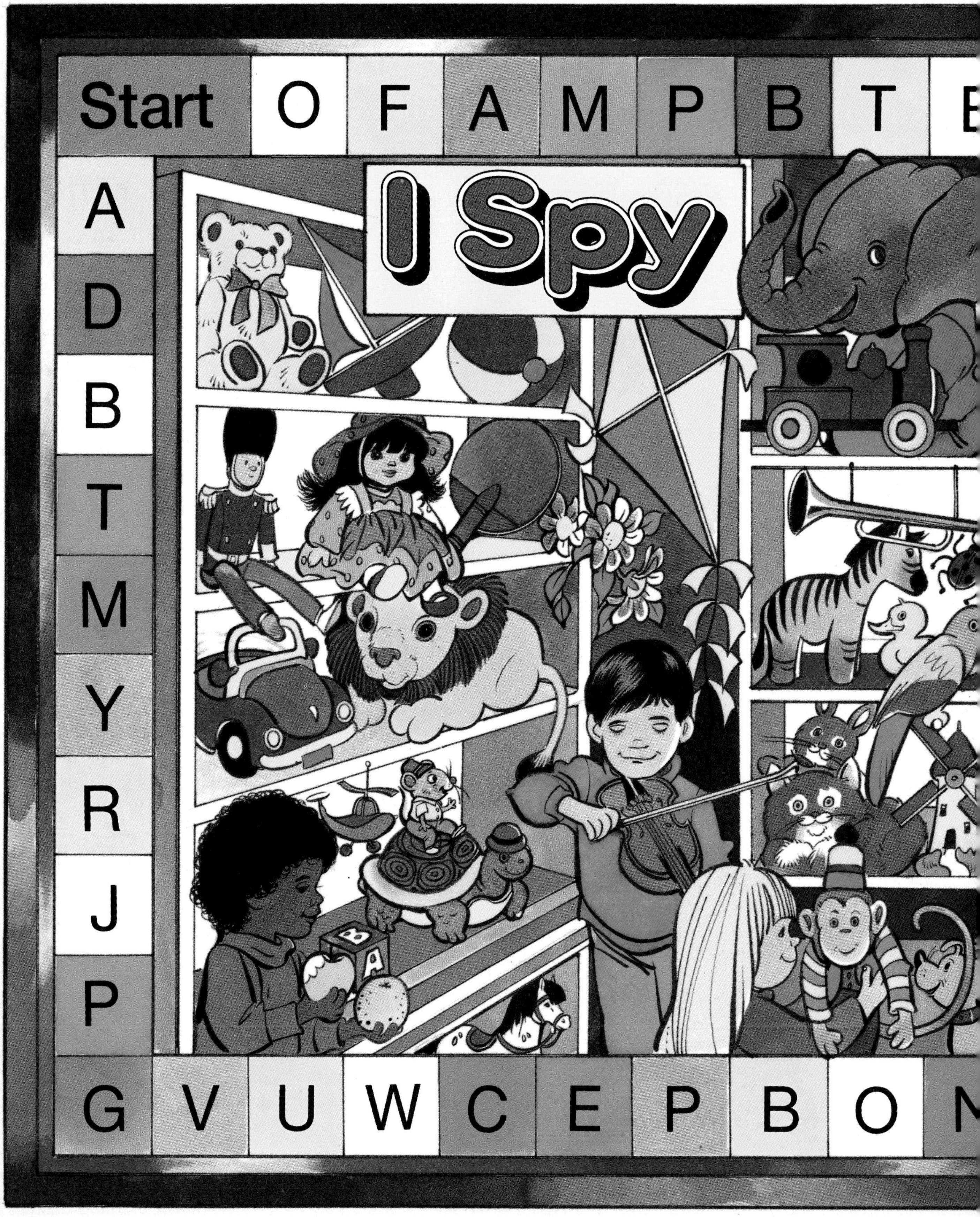

Start O F A M P B T E

A
D
B
T
M
Y
R
J
P

I Spy

G V U W C E P B O N

To play this game, roll a dice to see who goes first then set off round the track. Each time a player lands on a square, they have to spy something in the picture beginning with the letter in that square. If they can't find something, they're out of the game. No object can be "spied" twice. Keep going until there's only one person left — the winner!

Buttons

1 — Buttons and Mummy had arrived to collect Zoe from the playgroup. "Oh, dear! What's happened?" said Mummy. "Why are the children so upset?"

2 — Rosemary, the playgroup leader, told Mummy that the children's outing to the Christmas pantomime had been cancelled.

3 — Kind-hearted buttons felt sorry for her sister and the other girls and boys. She thought of an idea to cheer them up and told her teacher all about it next day at school.

4 — That evening, Mum phoned Rosemary about the plan. Soon, everything was arranged. Thank you, Mummy," beamed Buttons.

5 — Buttons was busy at school for the rest of the week. She worked hard every afternoon with her classmates, learning lines and rehearsing for a Christmas show.

6 — And a few nights later, she finished off one of her show costumes. Can you guess who Buttons is going to be?

7 — Cinderella, of course! Buttons' clever idea was to treat the playgroup children to a special afternoon performance of her school pantomime. Zoe and her friends had a wonderful time!

Sally and Scamp

C.C. RALLY

1 — Sally's best friend is her cheeky Shetland pony called Scamp. One day, Sally and her mum passed a caravan site.

2 — "What's that?" asked Sally, pointing to a sign. "It's a caravan club rally sign," said Mum.

3 — Sally said that a rally sounded fun. When they arrived home, she told Mum that she'd thought of a super idea.

4 — Later, Sally spent a long time making phone calls. Scamp wondered what was going on.

5 — That afternoon, Dad set up the barbecue in a corner of Scamp's field. "They'll be here soon," said Sally excitedly.

6 — A little later, Scamp heard the sound of hoofs clip-clopping along the road. It was Sally's chums arriving on their ponies.

7 — Clever Sally had arranged a pony rally. The boys and girls jumped over fences and played pony games . . .

8 — . . . then they enjoyed Dad's tasty burger buns and Mum's cakes. "This *is* fun," said Sally. And Scamp agreed!

Zebedee

ZEBEDEE was a Siamese cat,
Who lived down Primrose Lane.
His mistress was a little girl,
Whose name was Sarah Jane.

His fur was cream, his ears were brown,
His eyes were brightest blue,
And everywhere that Sarah went,
Her cat would be there, too.

He slept upon her bed at night,
Along with Teddy Bear.
He sat beside her dining chair,
And all her meals he'd share.

He rode inside her big dolls'pram,
He thought he was a king.
He danced around the room with her,
And even tried to sing.

He'd sit upon her knee and purr,
Or round her neck he'd curl.
They were a most devoted pair,
That Siamese cat and girl.

And then, one day, she went to school,
The cat, he could not go.
He sat outside the high school gate,
And howled his tale of woe.

At last, the bell rang, loud and clear,
And out came Sarah Jane.
Together she and Zebedee
Ran home to Primrose Lane.

The grumpy goblin

ONE snowy Christmas Eve, Santa Claus was having problems. His sleigh had broken down and the toys in his sack were getting bored.

"We should be on our way by now," grumbled Rosie the rag doll.

"Santa's going to be late with his deliveries," added Timmy the tin soldier.

"It's taking him ages to mend the sleigh," said Pippo the clown, yawning. "Can't we do something while we're waiting?"

"Let's go carol singing in Fir Tree Wood," suggested Rosie.

2 — "That's a super idea!" cried Timmy. "We'll sing to the animals!"

"We'd better ask Santa Claus first, though," said Pippo.

"Of course you may go," replied Santa smiling. "But don't wander far."

Carefully, the toys made their way across the snow-covered ground, until they reached a clearing in the wood.

As they began to sing, the little animals came out of their homes.

Mr and Mrs Squirrel and their babies were first, then Mr and Mrs Rabbit and their little ones hopped outside.

3 — The animals *were* pleased to hear the carols and sang along with the toys.

After a few minutes, however, a window opened in a tree trunk house nearby, and an angry face peered out.

"What a horrible din!" snapped a bad-tempered voice. "I'm trying to sleep!"

"Oh, it's only Grumps the goblin!" laughed Mr Rabbit. "Come on, Grumps — join in the carol singing!"

"Certainly not!" snorted the goblin. "It's cold out there and I'm sleepy."

"Oh, please, Grumps!" pleaded the baby squirrels. "Carol singing is fun."

"Oh, all right," grumbled Grumps, and he trudged out into the snow.

4 — And then, a strange thing happened . . . the animals stopped singing, and stared at a little fir tree which stood alone in the clearing.

"What's wrong?" asked Rosie.

"Our Christmas tree!" gasped Mrs Rabbit. "It's quite bare! Someone has taken all the decorations! Who would do such a thing?"

She turned to the toys.

"Every year, we dress up one of the little fir trees in the clearing," she explained. "It's our very own Christmas tree for *everyone* to share."

Just then, there was an embarrassed cough from Grumps, whose face had gone bright red!

5 — "It . . . was me," the goblin admitted quietly. "*I* took the decorations."

"But, why?" demanded Mr Squirrel. "The tree was for all of us to share."

"But you never share it with *me* !" sniffed Grumps. "Nobody's ever friendly with me, so I decided to have a tree of my own this year. I didn't have enough decorations, so I borrowed the ones belonging to you."

"That was very naughty of you, Grumps!" scolded Mrs Squirrel.

"I'm sorry," said Grumps sadly. "I'll go and fetch your decorations."

6 — "We'll help you!" offered the animals and toys.

Inside the goblin's house, his tree was sparkling and it looked beautiful!

"It does seem a pity to spoil the tree. You've decorated it so prettily, Grumps," sighed Mrs Squirrel.

"Yes," said Mr Rabbit. "And, it's late to start decorating another tree now."

"Well," suggested Grumps shyly. "Why don't you all come back to my house tomorrow? We can share Christmas Day — *and* the tree!"

"We'd love to!" said the animals.

7 — All at once, they heard a noise outside. It was Santa Claus looking for the toys.

"The sleigh's mended," he announced. "Hop aboard. There's no time to lose."

"Have a good time at the party, tomorrow!" cried the toys as they waved goodbye to their friends.

"I'm glad that ended happily," smiled Timmy, later.

"Me too," yawned Rosie.

All Pippo could do, however, was snore.

The bells on Santa's sleigh jingled as it sped through the frosty air.

Soon, Rosie and Timmy fell fast asleep, too . . . dreaming of Christmas morning and the happy children who would find them in their stockings.

Puzzle time

Emily has written her letter to Santa. Can you read what she has said to him?

Fill in the dotted areas to find one of the presents Emily would like.

Carefully study this line of Santas. Only *two* of them are *exactly* the same. Can you tell which they are?

Emily is hanging up her stocking. How many differences can you spot between the two pictures?

It's Christmas Day!
Help Emily find the fastest
way from her bed to the
presents under
the tree.

25
DEC.

In the wordsquare, look for everything that Santa
has left for Emily.

DOLL   BIKE   COT   GAMES   SWEET
TEDDY   PRAM   LIST   PAINTS   TOYS

B	T	M	A	R	P
I	S	E	M	A	G
K	I	C	D	T	T
E	L	L	O	D	O
S	W	E	E	T	Y
P	A	I	N	T	S

Join in the Christmas cheer by colouring the picture above with your paints or crayons.

Patch

1 — Paula Perkins and her kitten, Patch, were delighted to waken up one morning and discover it had been snowing! "Come on, Patch," said Paula excitedly. "Let's hurry up."

2 — Very soon, the pair were outside in the snow! "I'm going to make a snowman," said Paula, as Patch tried to catch snowflakes.

There are eight trophies hidden on these two pages. Can you find them?

3 — But, moments later, their fun was ruined when a huge dog frightened Patch, making him fall over in the snow. "Stop that at once!" said Paula. "This is *our* garden — you go back to your own one!"

4 — Poor Patch was so wet Paula had to carry him indoors and dry him off. "What a dreadful dog," she said.

5 — Once Patch was dried, the chums went back outside again. However, they'd only been out minutes when the nasty dog reappeared and annoyed Patch again.

6 — Shutting Patch safely in the house, Paula set to work. "I'll teach that dog a lesson he'll never forget," she said. "He's in for a shock!"

7 — And the next time the dog appeared in the garden looking for Patch, a shock is what he got! There, glaring at him, was a very fierce snow *cat*! "He thinks it's real," chuckled Paula.

My Baby Brother

WHILE heavy rain comes pouring down
In the house Ben huddles,
But once it stops, he runs outside
Splashing in the puddles.

When Ben looks through the window pane
To see a foggy day,
It puzzles him, because he thinks
The garden's gone away!

In winter, when the snow is deep
With softly fallen flakes,
Across the lawn, Ben loves to see
The footprints that he makes.

But far more fun than rain or snow
Ben loves a sunny day.
He splashes in his paddling pool —
The nicest games to play!

Let's look at Animals

THERE are 4500 species of mammals, more than one *million* types of insect, 20,000 varieties of fish and 8600 kinds of birds.

Here are some fascinating facts about just a few of them . . .

Why do *hyenas* laugh?

To let one another know where they are. They're not really laughing, just whooping loudly so that, in an emergency, they can group together.

Can *owls* see in the dark?

In total darkness, they can see nothing at all — they use their *ears* to find their prey. In dim light, however, they can see better than we do.

Why are *camels* born with hard skin on their feet?

To protect them from the hot desert sand. If you've ever walked on a sandy beach on a hot, sunny day, you'll know what it feels like!

Are *lions* lazy?

They doze for about 20 hours a day and leave most of the hunting to their lionesses — so do *you* think they're lazy?

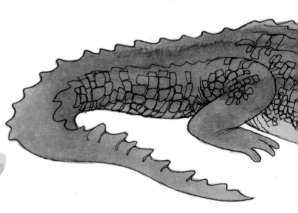

Which bird can fly backwards?

The *humming-bird*. It finds flying backwards useful when gathering nectar with its long beak. The world's smallest bird, it weighs less than 0.1 oz. All the humming-birds in the world, around 100,000, weigh only as much as a pair of ostriches!

Do *monkeys* have a good sense of smell?

No — but as they live in the treetops, it's not very important. Creatures which live on the ground need to be better sniffers — like the long-nosed spiny ant-eater (below).

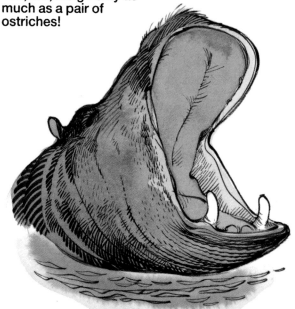

What does a *hippo* mean when it yawns?

It usually means trouble! Yawning is something a hippopotamus, which means "river horse", does when it's going to have a fight.

Does an *ostrich*, when faced with danger, hide its head in the sand?

No! When it feels threatened, the world's largest bird — which can't fly — lies down so flat it's hard to spot.

How does a *crocodile* carry its babies?

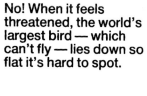

There is a small pouch inside the crocodile's mouth and it's in this that the young are carried.

Puzzle time

Spot the differences between the giraffes.

Hannah wants to reach her safari hut! Can you lead her there?

SWAMP

W	R	A	O	B	H
A	T	A	P	I	R
C	L	I	P	X	K
A	I	P	G	O	A
M	O	N	K	E	Y
S	N	A	K	E	R

MONKEY   HIPPO   TIGER
LION   YAK   BOAR   OX
TAPIR   SNAKE   MACAW

Try to find all these animals in the wordsquare.

Splish, Splash!

SARAH skipped merrily down the muddy lane searching for puddles to splash in. All the way, she sang,

"Splish, splash, splish,
Which puddle should I pick?
I want to splash in **all** of them
And give the leaves a kick!"

Then she squealed as she spotted a big deep puddle and took a huge leap into it.

"Look out, Sarah," cried her mum anxiously, "you might fall!"

But, the next moment, Sarah seemed to find herself falling deeper and deeper into the puddle.

2 — When she stopped spinning, Sarah found herself in a strange magical place. A girl was speaking to her.

"I'm Pam, the puddle princess," said the girl, "and I live in Cloud House. Why don't you come and play?"

3 — The puddle princess led Sarah through her house to the garden.

"There's no grass or flowers here," gasped Sarah. "Everything looks like clouds."

"Of course," said Pam, and she pulled on a big pair of blue wellies.

Sarah *was* puzzled but, before she could wonder what was going on, the puddle princess pulled her on to a cloud.

"Now, jump!" called Pam as she danced on the cloud. "It's just like jumping into puddles!"

4 — Sarah leapt up and down and discovered she was having fun.

"I knew you'd be good at this," laughed Pam. "I watched you splash in puddles."

Next, they jumped on darker clouds and Sarah was surprised to see water running out.

"We're making rain," explained Pam.

5 — Suddenly, she let out a piercing whistle.

At once, a rainbow appeared from nowhere and the girls ran to it.

6 — They played happily for hours, skipping over the rainbow and leaping on to clouds making it rain here, there and everywhere.

Then, when they were exhausted, the girls flopped down on a fluffy pink cloud.

"What fun we've had," sighed Sarah.

Then she added, "Race you to the rainbow!"

Sarah won, but then she slipped and started to slide down the rainbow.

The puddle princess just watched and waved goodbye.

7 — Sarah expected to feel herself falling through the sky so she shut her eyes.

Bump! She opened them and found herself sitting on the ground in the leafy lane where she'd left her mum and her puppy.

"Are you alright?" laughed Mum. "You slipped on the mud in the pool."

8 — "Oh," sighed Sarah sadly. "I must have imagined everything."

But, as she stared into the puddle, she was sure she saw Pam.

"She *is* real," grinned Sarah, skipping happily home.

Honey

1 — Honey and her friends decided to hold their very own Winter Games at Snowy Valley. They packed their sports gear and set off for some fun.

2 — "What shall we do first?" asked little Betsy Bear. "Let's start with a skating competition," suggested Honey. "Good idea," agreed her friends.

3 — But when Honey looked in her sports bag, she could only find *one* skate! "Oh, no! I've lost a skate!" she cried. And she missed the competition looking for it.

4 — As she lined up for the ski race, the sun shone in Honey's eyes. "Where are my sunglasses?" she wailed, reaching for them as Bobby waved the starting flag.

5 — The next event was a Snowman Building Contest. "I'll need my gloves for this," thought Honey, searching through her bag — but she didn't find them.

6 — Poor Honey had missed *all* the games. Her friends felt sorry for her. Then Billy Bear had a bright idea. "I know just the game for you, Honey," he chuckled.

7 — Billy told all the bears to close their eyes while he hid something. Then, a few moments later, he announced, "Our last winter game is Hunt the thimble!"

8 — To everyone's delight, Honey won easily. "I knew you could find it," laughed Billy. "You had plenty of practice *hunting* for things all day!" Honey *was* happy.

Family Fun

See how many Families you can collect in this super game! To play, shuffle the cards, then deal them to three or more players face down. The player on the dealer's left starts by asking any player for a card they need to complete a family.

If the player asked has the card, they must give it up. If not they say "NOT AT HOME". If the player gets the card they ask for, they can ask again, until they are told — "NOT AT HOME". The player who gives this reply goes next.

Keep playing until all the families are complete. The player with most complete sets at the finish is the winner.

Mr Rabbit

Mrs Rabbit

Miss Mouse

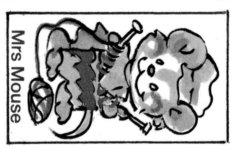
Mr Mouse

Master Rabbit

Master Mouse

Mrs Mouse

Miss Rabbit

Master Duck

Mr Duck

Mr Cat

Miss Duck

Mrs Duck

Mrs Cat

Mr Pig

Mr Squirrel

Miss Cat

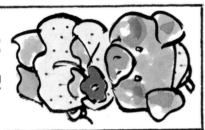

Mrs Pig

Mrs Squirrel

Master Cat

Master Pig

Miss Squirrel

Mr Hound

Miss Pig

Master Squirrel

Mrs Hound

Master Bear

Mr Bear

Master Hound

Miss Bear

Mrs Bear

Miss Hound

Fairy Fay

1 — Fairy Fay and her friends couldn't decide whether to go carol singing or sledging. "The snow is *perfect* for sledging," said Fay.

2 — "And we can go carol singing tonight, if we want to," replied Holly. So they joined in the fun with the other fairy children who were playing on the snowy slopes.

3 — "*Whee*!" cried the fairies excitedly, as the sledge travelled faster and faster. But suddenly it went out of control and crashed!

4 — Luckily, neither Fay nor her friends were hurt. They had, however, wakened up a little squirrel who had been hibernating in the tree. "*Brr*!" shivered the squirrel. "I'm cold!"

5 — The fairies were sorry that they had disturbed the squirrel and they brought him a nice warm jacket to wear. "Oh, thank you," he said gratefully as he put it on.

6 — Then, because he was very hungry, they searched the forest for some tasty fruit and nuts for their new friend to eat.

7 — And, later that afternoon, when the sleepy creature curled up again in his cosy bed of leaves, Fay and her friends found themselves singing after all — a lullaby to help him fall fast asleep.

How to make...
Santa's Grotto

Paste these two pages to card then make a window to look through by carefully cutting along the red dotted lines on this page.

Cut out Santa's elves and slot them on their bases.

Cut out these figures, too, to stand outside the grotto.

Fold

Fold

Fold

Fold

Fold

Fold

Now make the background for the grotto by cutting all round the red dotted lines on this page. Fold the two top strips of card over twice as shown.

Stick or tape the small squares of card to the back of the window. Finally fold the base of the background scene along the dotted line, and arrange the figures around the grotto.

Penny Crayon

1 — Penny and her chums found painters in the school gym. "What about our class?" they sighed.

2 — But whatever Penny drew with her special crayons became *real*, so she began drawing books on the classroom wall.

3 — Miss Fitt, the gym teacher, was *not* amused, however. "Enough!" she called. "You can't behave like this!"

4 — Penny drew Liz McCloggan, the famous athlete. But *she* made everyone work really hard. "*This* is no fun," wailed the class.

5 — Penny quickly rubbed out the runner. "I've thought of a way we can have both exercise *and* fun," she cried.

6 — Penny turned the gym into a jungle! "This is more like it," her classmates whooped as they scrambled up the trees.

Join Penny by colouring in this picture with your paints or crayons.

©MADDOCKS

Storyworld

Start

1

2

3

Given a magic carpet ride by Aladdin. Fly on 4 spaces.

4

5

6

Stop to help look for little Thumbelina. Go back 2 spaces.

7

8

Miss a turn while you join Snow White and the Seven Dwarves for tea.

9

10

11

12

13

14

Climb up tower on Rapunzel's hair, then swing across to 17.

To play this game, trace or cut out the counters on the facing page. Then throw a dice to see who starts. First to the finish is the winner.

The witch's spells

1 Go back to 10. 2 Miss a turn. 3 Go to Finish. 4 Move back 4 places. 5 Start again. 6 Move back 5 places.

16

17

18

You meet Red Riding Hood's grandmother — or is it the wolf? Run back 6 places.

19

20

You go swimming with the Little Mermaid. Miss a turn.

21

22

23

24

25

You're invited to ride in Cinderella's coach. Go on 2 places.

A witch puts a spell on you. Throw a dice then follow her instructions above.

26

27

28

Finish

The End

I'm buying Molly and Monty Mouse their Xmas presents. Skates . . .

. . . and a basin!

Carrie

Good! Molly and Monty *are* pleased with their skates.

Now, fill the basin with water . . .

. . . let it freeze — and they have their own ice rink!

Puzzle time

Can you tell which silhouette figure exactly matches the dancing puppet?

Join the dots to see what these puppets are doing!

The five puppets on the right look similar but only two of them are wearing the very same. Which are they?

The puppets below are forming the letters that make up the name of the puppeteer. Rearrange them to discover what it is.

ANSWER —
SOPHIE

You can colour this picture.

Can you find where the small coloured squares fit?

Try to find the six hidden cat faces.

How many items begin with the letter "p"?

Which Witch?

MOONSHINE the witch was annoyed with Furryfeet and Croaker.

"You never help me with the cooking, you won't even try to learn how to make spells," she scolded.

"I'd rather snooze. Who wants to make spells?" purred Furryfeet the cat.

"I'd rather play. I can't be bothered learning!" croaked Croaker the frog.

Then, Moonlight caught sight of her grumpy face in the mirror.

"I don't like being a witch — I'm tired of rat stew and living in this old cottage in the forest. I'd rather be someone else," she decided.

2 — Later, she heard that the prince from Cherry Hill Palace was searching for a lady-in-waiting for his bride.

"That would suit me!" declared Moonshine. "But the prince wouldn't want an ugly witch as a lady-in-waiting . . ."

She quickly opened her spell book and chanted spell number five.

"Fiddledy, faddledy, fidgety fee,
Make me as beautiful as can be!"

The spell worked perfectly!

However, Furryfeet and Croaker didn't like the new Moonshine.

"We liked you the way you were before," they cried.

3 — Then they heard the sound of carriage wheels bumping along the forest path.

The three of them ran to look. It was the prince from the palace!

He took one look at Moonshine and invited her to be his bride's lady-in-waiting!

She didn't see Furryfeet and Croaker waving sadly as she disappeared from view.

4 — Moonshine loved living at Cherry Hill Palace. The prince and princess were kind to her, she was given lovely clothes to wear and delicious food to eat.

She never thought of Furryfeet and Croaker — not until one night when a terrible thunderstorm broke overhead.

Moonshine's room was very dark and she could hear the rain on her window.

"Poor Furryfeet and Croaker," thought Moonshine. "They were always terrified of thunderstorms. I wonder if they're all right?"

Suddenly, Moonshine felt rather homesick. She got out of bed and went to look out of the window at the storm. Just then, there was a big flash of lightning and Moonshine caught sight of herself in the mirror — and what a shock she had!

5 — Instead of golden curls, a silky nightdress, and pink slippers, she had long, straggly hair, a witch's dress and hobnail boots.

Moonshine had changed back!

"Oh, no!" she wailed. "I can't let the prince and princess see me like this — but I can't remember how to do spell number five, either. Why has the spell stopped working?"

Sadly, Moonshine realised that the only place for a witch like her was back in the forest.

6 — She trudged wearily through the forest and finally she reached her old cottage. On the door a banner read,

"WELCOME HOME, MOONSHINE!"

"How did they know I'd be back?" puzzled Moonshine.

Furryfeet and Croaker were delighted to see her.

"We've missed you!" purred Furryfeet, winding himself round her legs.

"It's good to have you back!" added Croaker, leaping up joyfully.

"It's good to see you, too!" yawned Moonshine, who flopped down into a chair and fell fast asleep.

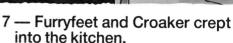

7 — Furryfeet and Croaker crept into the kitchen.

On the table lay a book called *How To Turn Someone Back Again.*

"We did it! Our very first spell worked!" giggled the pair.

"We'll tell Moonshine when she wakes up!" said Croaker.

"And we'll both help more with the spells and the cooking in future," added Furryfeet. "We don't want to give Moonshine a reason to go away again."

And Moonshine? She was still asleep dreaming of when she was someone else.

Twinkle

is on sale Every Wednesday

Packed with stories, puzzles, competitions, things to do.

Now look and see if you guessed correctly, before trying to find where the figures shown in the box are on this page.

HAPPY CHRISTMAS